ANIMAL FOLK SONGS FOR CHILDREN

BOOKS BY RUTH CRAWFORD SEEGER

AMERICAN FOLK SONGS FOR CHILDREN

ANIMAL FOLK SONGS FOR CHILDREN

Music Editor for

OUR SINGING COUNTRY by John A. and Alan Lomax

FOLK SONG: U. S. A. by John A. and Alan Lomax

Linnet Books

Animal
Folk Songs for
Children

TRADITIONAL AMERICAN SONGS

by Ruth Crawford Seeger

ILLUSTRATED BY BARBARA COONEY

Hamden, Connecticut 1993

First published 1993 as a Linnet Book,
an imprint of
The Shoe String Press, Inc., Hamden, Connecticut 06514.

Library of Congress Cataloging-in-Publication Data

Animal folk songs for children : traditional American songs
[compiled] by Ruth Crawford Seeger ;
illustrated by Barbara Cooney.
1 score. With piano acc. and chord symbols.
Reprint. Originally published: Garden City, N.Y. :
Doublday, © 1950.
Summary: A collection of forty American folk songs about all
kinds of animals, including "Black Sheep, Black Sheep,"
"Oh, Blue," and "Cross-eyed Gopher."
1. Children's songs.   2. Folk music—United States.
3. Folk songs, English—United States.
4. Animals—Songs and music.
[1. Folk songs—United States.   2. Animals—Songs and music.]
I. Seeger, Ruth Crawford, 1901–1953.
II. Cooney, Barbara, 1917–   . ill.
M1997.A558   1992   92-767692
ISBN 0–208–02364–X (cloth)   ISBN 0–208–02365–8 (pbk.)

The paper in this book meets the minimum requirements of
American National Standard for Information Sciences—
Permanence of Paper for Printed Library Materials,
ANSI Z39.48–1984.

Printed in the United States of America

Sources and Acknowledgments

Of the forty-three songs in this book, thirty-four are fresh notations from traditional singing: two, direct from singers; thirty-two, from field recordings in the Archive of American Folk Song in the Library of Congress in Washington. The remaining nine songs are re-printed from folklore publications.

Of the thirty-two songs, six to my knowledge had previously been notated from the same singer's recording and published elsewhere. Reasons for choosing these versions rather than others not previously published are too various to detail here. Reasons for wishing to re-transcribe rather than re-print can be mentioned briefly. It is important that a folksong not be frozen in any one standard variant or version: that there not come to be one "right" way to sing a folksong — even though different ways make group singing a problem at times! It is also important that we be reminded of variation in traditional singing. I have therefore gone to the recordings of these few songs with the purpose of choosing when possible one of the singer's variants other than that already in print. The amount of variation differs among singers. In "Hop Up, My Ladies", it is negligible; in "Mole in the Ground", extensive. The collections in which these songs were first published have been included among the Acknowledgments, with an asterisk marking the song-title.

Acknowledgment is made to the following publishers, societies, institutions and individuals, for permission to use the songs as indicated:

AMERICAN FOLKLORE SOCIETY (The Journal of American Folklore) *"My Old Hen's a Good Old Hen"; "Turkey Song" ("As I Came Over Yonders Hill") in Kentucky Folksong in Northern Wisconsin, Asher E. Treat, Vol. 52, Jan.-Mar., 1939.

COTTEN, ELIZABETH, singer: "The Old Cow Died" (notated by the author).

CREIGHTON, HELEN: *"The Crocodile Song", Songs and Ballads from Nova Scotia, J. B. Dent and Sons, copyright, 1932.

FISCHER, CARL: *"I Wish I Wuz a Mole in the Ground", 30 and 1 Folk Songs from the Southern Mountains, Bascom Lamar Lunsford and Lamar Stringfield, copyright, 1929.

HALPERT, HERBERT, collector: "Little Dog Named Right" (notated by Violeta Halpert from the singing of Morner Bowden).

HARCOURT, BRACE AND COMPANY: "Little Black Bull" ("Hoosen Johnny"), The American Songbag, Carl Sandburg, copyright, 1927.

HARVARD UNIVERSITY PRESS: "Mister Rabbit" (st. 5, AAFS 3044 B1); "A Squirrel is a Pretty Thing" (from "Pain in My Fingers", p. 167), On the Trail of Negro Folk Songs, Dorothy Scarborough, (reprinted by permission of the publishers), copyright, 1925.

HOOSIER FOLKLORE SOCIETY and Hoosier Folklore: quotation from Tales from the Ozark Hills, Vance Randolph, Vol. IX, Apr.-June, 1950.

LOMAX, JOHN A. and ALAN: *"Hop Up, My Ladies", Our Singing Country, The MacMillan Company, copyright, 1941.

MACMILLAN COMPANY, THE: *"Riding Round the Cattle" ("The Old Chisholm Trail"), Cowboy Songs, John A. and Alan Lomax, copyright, 1938; *"Stewball", American Ballads and Folk Songs, John A. and Alan Lomax, copyright, 1934.

MUSIC PUBLISHERS' JOURNAL: "Snake Baked A Hoecake", in American Folksong and the Total Culture, Jacob A. Evanson, July-Aug., Sept.-Oct., 1944.

STATE HISTORICAL SOCIETY OF MISSOURI: "The Old Sow" ("The Measles in the Spring") and "There Was an Old Frog" (two variants combined in accordance with collector's notes), Ozark Folk-

songs, Vance Randolph, Vols. III (copyright, 1949) and II (copyright, 1948).

UNIVERSITY OF MICHIGAN PRESS: "Animal Song," *Ballads and Songs of Southern Michigan,* Emelyn Elizabeth Gardner and Geraldine Jencks Chickering, copyright, 1939.

UNIVERSITY OF MISSOURI: "And We Hunted and We Hunted" ("Three Jolly Welshmen"), *Ballads and Songs,* edited by H. M. Belden, 1940.

... and to the LIBRARY OF CONGRESS and the ARCHIVE OF AMERICAN FOLK SONG, and the collectors and singers of the following songs transcribed from field recordings obtainable from the Archive[1]:

CREIGHTON, HELEN, collector: "Crocodile Song," Edmund Henneberry.

DRAVES, ROBERT F., collector: "My Old Hen's a Good Old Hen," Mrs. Pearl Jacobs Borusky.

HALPERT, HERBERT, collector: "The Big Sheep," Austin Harmon (st. 6, Lomax, *Our Singing Country,* p. 105); "Cross-eyed Gopher," Thaddeus C. Willingham; "Little Brown Dog," Mrs. Birmah Hill Grissom; "Muskrat," Austin Harmon; "Oh, Blue," the Scruggs family; "Old Ground Hog," Austin Harmon (st. 8, 9, from AAFS 2852 A1; st. 11, from AAFS 302 A1); "Wolves a-Howling," John Hatcher.

LOMAX, JOHN A. and ALAN, collectors: "Black Sheep, Black Sheep," Drew Howard ("flitting round" substituted for "picking out"): "Daddy Shot a Bear," Annie Brewer; "Go On, Old 'Gator," Augustus Haggerty and group (alt. refrain from AAFS 3093 A3); "Go to Sleepy," Florida Hampton; "The Gray Goose," Washington (Lightnin'), (st. 10, 11, 13, 16, 17, 18, 21 from AAFS 223 A2; st. 19, 20, Lomax, *American Ballads and Folk Songs*); "Hop Up, My Ladies" ("Hop Light, My Ladies"), Fields Ward; "Jack, Can I Ride?," Ed Jones (st. 2, *Journal of American Folk Lore,* Vol. 61, p. 48); "Little Lapdog Lullaby," Vera Hall; "Of All the Beast-es," J. L. Goree (st. 2, Mary Ann James); "Old Bell'd Yoe" ("Old Bell Ewe and the Little Speckled Wether"), T. G. Hoskins; "Old Fox" ("Old Mother Hippletoe"), J. D. Dillingham (st. 10 composite of several variants, Vance Randolph, *Ozark Folk-songs,* Vol. I, pp. 386-90); "Old Hen Cackled and Rooster Laid an Egg," Arthur Armstrong (st. 3, 4, Mary Ann James); "Old Lady Goose," Irene Williams; "Peep, Squirrel," Hettie Godfrey (st. 5, 7, 8, Celina Lewis); "Raccoon and Possum" ("Fortune"), tune sung by Fields Ward, st. 1, 2, 4 from dictation, "Rove, Riley, Rove," J. G. Willingham; "Riding Round the Cattle" ("Ti-yiddle-um-yeah"), Mose Platt ("Old Chisholm Trail" stanzas from Lomax, *Cowboy Songs* and *American Ballads and Folk Songs*); "Shake That Little Foot, Dinah-o" (Shake That Wooden Leg, Dinah-o"), Mrs. Minta Morgan (st. 1, 2, 4, 5 adapted from "Ole Aunt Dinah," Scarborough, *On the Trail of Negro Folk Songs,* pp. 187-88); "Stewball," group in Oakley, Miss., AAFS 1855 A (st. 6, 7, Lomax *American Ballads and Folk Songs*); "Whoa, Mule, Can't Get the Saddle On," Celina Lewis.

MOSER, ARTUS, collector: "The Deer Song" ("On a Bright and Summer's Morning"), Bascom Lamar Lunsford (st. 2-8, Lomax, *Our Singing Country*), p. 103.

ROBERTSON (COWELL), SIDNEY, collector: "Mole in the Ground," Bascom Lamar Lunsford.

SONKIN, ROBERT and TODD, CHARLES L., collectors: "The Kicking Mule," the King family; "Little Pig" ("Man and Woman Bought a Little Pig") Mrs. Vernon Shafter.

I would like to express appreciation to many other people whose names cannot be included in these pages. Very special gratitude is due to Glenore Horne, Herbert Halpert, Sidney Robertson Cowell and Rae Korson, Reference Assistant at the Archive of American Folk Song, who have contributed generously of their time and thought during the making and editing of the book. And to John and Alan Lomax, in collaboration with whom I made my first thorough acquaintance with American folk idioms. And always to my husband Charles Seeger and the four children who have come to know how much time it takes a mother to make a book.

[1]The singer's name follows the song title. Archive numbers are given only with supplementary stanzas, or when no singer's name is available.

Contents

Alphabetical Song Contents

Introduction

Children naturally like animals, feel close to them, want to hear all about them. Folk singers like animals too, and like to sing about them. They have sung these songs with children in many places over long periods of time. The accumulated affection which generations of singers have felt for child, animal, and song shines through their singing, and must claim large credit for the warmth and vitality of these songs.

Animals in American folk song incline more toward the carefree than the introspective. They seldom moralize or give even indirect social or political comment, as did so many folk beast tales in Greece and India over two thousand years ago, yet both children and adults can distill wisdom in plenty from the ways these animals think and act in song. Like a friendly visiting uncle (one of the family but not bearer of its responsibilities), they feel free to observe, tease, comfort, give advice, scold a little, make wishes, jest loud or delicately, tell stories true or nonsensical — and make up monstrously unbelievable lies.

Says one Missouri tall-tale teller of another: "Folks used to say he was the champion liar of the whole country. But them tales of his wasn't really lies, and everybody knowed it. They was just big windy stories. . . ." American singers also like to fill their songs with whoppers that aren't really lies — exaggerations so obviously incredible that anyone who feels need to boast may let himself go without restraint. There is lusty lying about size, as in "The Crocodile Song" or "The Big Sheep" (a "Ram of Darby" version is said to have been George Washington's favorite song). There is fantastic lying, as in "Little Brown Dog" or "The Deer Song" (seventeen lies in thirteen stanzas, children triumphantly count). There is the lying which is more like a wish to believe in something, as in "The Gray Goose."

And there are varying degrees all along the way from the unbelievable to the believable — from the really huge whoppers through all the kinds of lesser nonsense and comments on the facts and happenings of a day's living, and on to such songs of wonderful people among animals as "Oh, Blue" or "Stewball." If you feel warmly toward animals (even the rascally ones), you may find it hard to say what is nonsense, what is wisdom, what is believable.

Rabbits are everywhere, and ready with answers: nuisances generally, but how can you be angry with someone when you are singing to him? Raccoon talks to the possum, and the possum talks to man. Man scolds the muskrat, for muskrat stole his corn — but everyone must eat, even muskrats, and it's affectionate scolding. The fox raids the barnyard and makes away with the goose — but, after all, he is only feeding his young. The alligator is given orders to go back to his hole — but he's sung about as one of God's creatures. On the farm are hens, roosters, pigs, sheep, an occasional turkey — each with something to contribute of nonsense or wisdom or fact. Dogs and horses are favorites among songs, as in real life. And always there is the mule. Somewhere along the line the elephant stepped out of the circus and entered folk tradition, together with the panther and the bear. But they are lonely. Other zoo animals, like the lion, the giraffe, and zebra (so frequently seen in school textbooks) are still foreigners to an American folk singer's repertoire. As for the fish and the birds and the small things, they are quite at home — so plentiful, in fact, that (except for two) they will have to wait for a book of their own.

In choosing traditional songs for children and families and teachers to enjoy, many questions arise. What is a folk song? How have folk songs been found and gathered? If you cannot gather them yourself,

9

out among the singers, is it better to seek them through reading (in printed collections of folk material) or through listening (to phonograph recordings of traditional singing)? Where do you find such recordings? And how do you go about choosing from among so many songs?

Even folklorists disagree when defining a folk song. Perhaps we might say it is a kind of song not known to have been composed by any one person, a song handed down over the years from singer to singer without aid of print, a song containing within itself some of the character and history and custom of the people who have sung it, a song willing to change along the way of its travel according to the needs or creativeness of any particular singer or group.

Folk songs are found and gathered in various ways. Some collectors have notated them with pencil and paper, direct from the singer. Others have recorded them on the old Edison cylinders, on discs, tape, or on wire. Some collectors stay close at home, finding songs in their own or nearby yards, streets, kitchens, grocery stores — around their own or neighboring firesides. Others have gone out and up and down to inaccessible places, hauling bulky recording equipment to far-off cabins and lonely fields, spending all night of many nights recording the thread of a singer's remembering, or traveling hundreds of zig-zag miles from town to town trailing an itinerant singer who (somebody said) was a good singer of good songs but who didn't stay put. Some of these recordings, known as field recordings, are in private collections. Many thousands of others have been deposited as master discs in the Archive of American Folk Song at the Library of Congress; duplicates of most of them may be purchased.

Listening over many years to such recordings, I have come to feel that *the way* folk singers sing and play their music is almost as important as the music itself. Those of us who have not grown up with music like this cannot really get to know it through a printed page. We need to hear it. We must remember, of course, that many field recordings are made under difficult conditions — sometimes miles away from electric current, in mountain houses, along country roads, in town barrooms or restaurants, at church services or noisy dances. It is natural that they vary widely in quality and clarity of tone, tune, and text. We must remember also that any unaccustomed language (or music) may sound strange at first. Some listeners are ready to like strange things. Others may need closer acquaintance and longer listening before coming to enjoy such qualities in this music as its epic objectivity, its refusal to act chameleon to word meanings or moods, its rough vitality, its monotony. The listener must bring an unprejudiced ear to all manner of voices, being ready to welcome — perhaps eventually to prefer — some splintery ones, some nasal, some unaccompanied ones, pitches slipping and sliding at traditionally right places in a tune (which often are quite different from what we might expect).

Listening of this sort can yield an enjoyment and understanding which reading of notes or words cannot give.

It is from field recordings — from the voices of the singers — that I have chosen most of the songs in this book. The selecting of a hundred or so song titles from among the many thousand in the Archive's lists and files is a story in itself — an adventure over wide expanses of a large country, seeing the way songs have of moving around and parting and meeting again, without actually hearing the voices of the people who sing. And then, when finally the records are listened to and many of the songs notated, the choosing of a few from among them is still another adventure.

Some songs are easy to choose. Here's "Cross-eyed Gopher", with banjo figures to use as piano interludes. Here's "Wolves a-Howling," with interwoven song tune and fiddle tune (and let's try separating them as part of the song's piano accompaniment). "Old Fox" is an immediate "yes," in the light of a score of other variants we know. Discovering "Little Brown Dog" is a thing to remember, one evening; "Little Lap-Dog Lullaby," another; and "Old Bell'd Yoe," with its fiddle figures for piano playing; and, early one morning, a panther song from Texas (but our housekeeper, Mary Ann Benford James, comes listening, says she grew up in Alabama with a song like that, and chants another stanza from her childhood).

Some songs are harder to choose. Often a song has many versions or variants. One folk singer is likely to differ from another in singing a song; moreover, he may vary his own tune from one stanza to another. How do you choose from among so many ways of singing a song? Which singer's version do you choose, and why? And then which of that singer's variants shall you choose as the representative tune to be crystallized in print and to mean thereafter that song to many people? When nine singers come along on recordings singing nine variants of "Old Ground Hog," to be added to the other variants you know, which shall be chosen? The most typical, the most unique, the easiest for children to sing, or the one you like best? And when several versions of "Old Chisholm Trail" have become familiar to a large public through books and commercial recordings, shall one of these be used? Or shall horizons be stretched and a more unique relative be chosen — less familiar but too nice to be little known?

I must admit that in the choosing of the various songs I have at times been drawn in each of these directions, and occasionally in all directions at once. Some of the songs are typical, some unique; most of them are fresh notations of versions not to my knowledge previously published.

Thus a family-and-children's song book has developed a dual character and become, surprisingly enough, a sort of folklore source book as well. It has found itself seeking to bring together two values which often travel apart: research value and practical use value. It presents itself alike to students of folklore (whose enjoyment of a "new" song or version includes interest in its authenticity, its source, and the faithfulness of its notation) and to people who like to sing (who may or may not care about authenticity, but who want to learn the song, play it, enjoy using it).

All texts—as, of course, all tunes—are traditional. (See pages 5, 6, for further data.) Suggestions for improvising on the words of songs have been given in *American Folk Songs for Children*. These animal songs are of the same sort, grew out of similar environments, may be used comfortably in similar ways. A few of them tell a story, with a correct place to begin and end. But more often they are songs which begin in the middle of things — "now" rather than "then"; which have no special right place for starting or stopping; which welcome improvisation as part of their growth, encouraging bedtime sessions to stretch too long or singing at school to overflow its time.

Groups of children singing "The Old Cow Died" will do as the traditional singer did when she was a child in North Carolina: "We just kept on jigging and dancing and making up more things. We sang it different each time." "Whoa, Mule" goes on a long time or short, depending on the children and the mule. There is always one more part of Mister Rabbit's anatomy to sing about. And when "panther" (pronounced "panner" in both variants) sounds like "camel" on the Texas recording, why not sing also about a camel?

> *Of all the beast-es in the world*
> *I'd rather be a camel.*
> *I'd crawl into some desert land*
> *And cry for Susianna.*

The pleasure of belonging to a song through making up new words can come to be so strong that the older traditional words are left off in a corner, neglected or forgotten — more by accident than by intention. We must remember that both the old and the new are essential to a folk song's staying alive — that, although the song grows and spreads partly through its ability to gather fresh experiences from whatever is happening around it will lose its identity if these new elements crowd out or obliterate the old. Let's suppose the song is a passenger train, with tune as engine and stanzas as cars. You can add any number of coaches of different kinds. You can even add a few freight cars. But if too many freight cars are added, the passenger train becomes a freight train — with quite a different character, and probably with a different destination.

In making sure we keep some of the old and traditional while feeling free to add the new, we should be aware not only of words and tunes but of *ways* of singing and playing. For certain habits and traditions in the singing and playing of this music can scarcely be separated from the song without loss to the song. Some of these habits show a basic difference from habits and traditions in our fine art and popular music.

Folk singing is devoid of platform self-consciousness and "graces." The singer just sings, as though by himself or among relations or neighbors. He sings in natural singing voice, with neither undue pride nor apology for its quality. He shows no hesitation in letting his voice carry the song unaccompanied. He sings fairly fast, seldom dragging even when the words are tragic or meditative. His metrical beat (or pulse) is strong and frequent. Music is not used as a means to dramatizing the words. There is no urgent seeking for variety, no "expression," no slowing up at ends of stanzas or songs, no increase or decrease in loudness for special effect.

Folk accompaniment shows similar habits. The banjo and guitar and string band are uninfluenced by shifting moods of the song. Once they set a degree of speed or loudness they maintain it until the song ends. If the piano is to be used in accompanying folk songs it should keep as many of the qualities of traditional accompaniment as possible. In adopting a song it should adopt some of the song's habits — and adjust some of its own habits to those of the song. The piano is more accustomed to being a solo than a subordinate instrument. It can easily be too noisy or too resonant for the usual singing voice. Rich edifices of sound, natural to it, are not natural to folk songs. The damper pedal can muddy the clarity of a brisk bass. A heavy left hand can make perky figures seem dull. Perhaps best in the bass, especially with lively songs, is either a staccato or a semi-staccato tone: as though played on a banjo or guitar, "picked" but not dainty, "dry" but not wooden. In fast songs the pedal should not be used; in others, sparingly. If the pianist "chords" by ear he should choose simple triads, preferring them thin (with few tones) rather than thick (with too many). If the written accompaniment contains melodic reminders of banjo or guitar figures, he should allow them to be heard in conversation with the song tune. As for short slurs of a few notes, they are salt, pepper, and spice in music, especially if given good accent on their initial tones.

Chord letters have been placed above the staff line of each song in the book, as a help to pianists who like to make their own accompaniments, and to players of other instruments which sound well with folk songs — the guitar, banjo, auto-harp, ukulele, the accordion. These letters are suggestions only: different chord patterns are often possible. A chapter on Accompaniment in *American Folksongs for Children* makes further suggestions, and provides a music chart of the most used scales and their primary chords. Traditional players use very few basic chords, and keep the same one without change as long as the tune will allow. Out of this chordal monotony they make music which has motion, continuity, steadiness of beat, melodic variety — and a feeling of belonging to the song. The pianist, in chording, must find his own way of balancing between monotony and variety. Above all, when singing with a group, he must be at ease with his instrument. He should never allow it to keep him so busy that he subordinates the song to its accompaniment, loses the flow of the tune, slows the speed, or interrupts the pulse.

Perhaps most characteristic among the traditions of this music, and most important for us to retain as we sing and play it, is the keeping going, the insistent moving on, the maintaining of pulse and pace and mood unbroken throughout the singing of a song. Songs are sung as though they might continue off into space. This singing and playing is close accompaniment to living: to working, to playing games, to dancing all night, to doing nothing, to doing anything a long time, to jogging down a night road behind the unhurried clop-clop of the old mare's hoofs, or riding along in a car or truck with miles rolling away underneath. In making the piano accompaniments for this book this keep-goingness, or never-endingness, has been a thing cherished. The last measure of a song has often been left up in the air, with no final home chord (tonic) tempting the player to ritard or to stop and pay homage to the approaching double bar. It is hoped that such avoidance of tonal finality will help the player feel this last measure not as an ending but as part of a continuing song; that it will pull him past the double bar he has been taught to observe as stop sign, and on back to the beginning *without loss of the song's speed or pulse.* And, when at last it really comes time to stop, perhaps (having no comfortably padded home chord to relax into) he may find he likes taking leave of a song as folk singers do — casually, as though soon to meet again.

THE SONGS

Raccoon and Possum

VIRGINIA and MISSISSIPPI

Fast ♩ = 120

Rac-coon's got a ring-round tail, Pos-sum tail goes bare, The

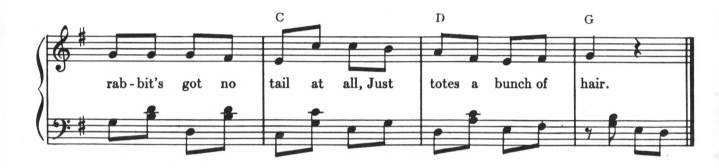

rab-bit's got no tail at all, Just totes a bunch of hair.

2. The raccoon is a mighty man,
   He rambles through the dark,
   You ought to see him hunt his den
   When he hears old Ranger bark.

3. Possum up the 'simmon tree,
   Raccoon on the ground,
   Raccoon says to the possum,
   "Won't you shake them 'simmons down?"

4. I met that possum in the road,
   "Possum, where you gwine?"
   "Look out, man, don't bother me,
   I'm hunting muscadine."

5. Rabbit up the gum-stump,
   Cooney in the hollow,
   Possum in the 'tater patch
   As fat as he can wallow.

Mister Rabbit

VIRGINIA

Mis-ter Rab-bit, Mis - ter Rab-bit, your ears might-y long,

Yes, my Lawd, they're put on wrong.

REFRAIN

Ev - ery lit-tle soul must shine, shine, shine,

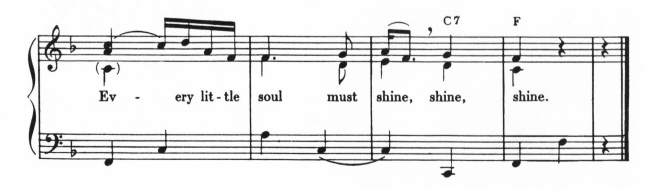

Ev - ery lit-tle soul must shine, shine, shine.

2. Mister Rabbit, Mister Rabbit, your coat mighty gray.
   Yes, my Lawd, 'twas made that way.

   REFRAIN:
   Every little soul must shine, shine, shine,
   Every little soul must shine, shine, shine.

3. Mister Rabbit, Mister Rabbit, your feet mighty red,
   Yes, my Lawd, I'm almost dead.
   Refrain:

4. Mister Rabbit, Mister Rabbit, your tail mighty white.
   Yes, my Lawd, and I'm a-getting out of sight.
   Refrain:

5. Mister Rabbit, Mister Rabbit, you look mighty thin.
   Yes, my Lawd, been cutting through the wind.
   Refrain:

Peep Squirrel

Moderately fast ♩ = 100

Peep,__squirrel, dah dah did-dle-um, Peep, squirrel, dah__ dle dah did-dle-um,
Walk,__squirrel, dah dah did-dle-um, Walk, squirrel, dah__ dle dah did-dle-um,

well accented

Peep, squirrel, dah dah did-dle-um, Peep, squirrel, dah__ dle dah did-dle-um
Walk, squirrel, dah dah did-dle-um, Walk, squirrel, dah__ dle dah did-dle-um.

3. Jump, squirrel, dah dah diddle-um,
   Jump, squirrel, dah-dle dah diddle-um. *(Repeat)*

4. Skip, squirrel, dah dah diddle-um, *etc.*

5. Run, squirrel, dah dah diddle-um, *etc.*

6. Fly, squirrel, dah dah diddle-um, *etc.*

7. Catch the squirrel, dah dah diddle-um, *etc.*

8. Caught the squirrel, dah dah diddle-um, *etc.*

In Alabama this is played as a chasing game. Two squirrels are behind two posts. They peep, walk, jump, skip, in any order dictated by the song. When the running begins, the squirrel who is "it" starts chasing the other. Sometimes the song goes on to killing and cooking.

A Squirrel Is a Pretty Thing

A squir-rel is a pret-ty thing, He car-ries a pret-ty tail,

ARKANSAS

He eats all the farm-er's corn And husks it on the rail.

Cross-eyed Gopher

Fast ♩ = 144
INTERLUDE 1 (banjo)
Play twice

MISSISSIPPI

STANZA

Hey, _____ cross-eyed go-pher, punch him in the ribs, and he'll turn o-ver.

INTERLUDE 2 (banjo)
Play twice

Muskrat

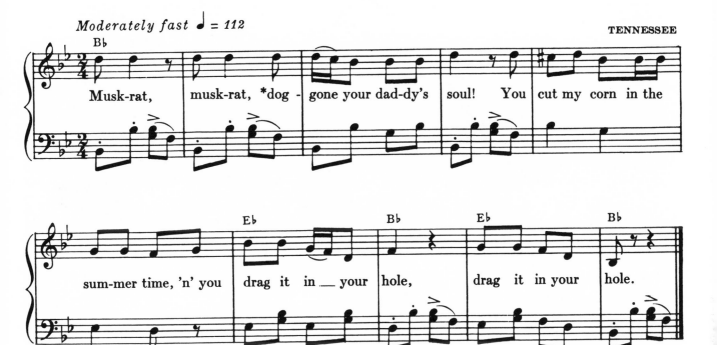

Moderately fast ♩ = 112

Musk-rat, musk-rat, *dog - gone your dad-dy's soul! You cut my corn in the sum-mer time, 'n' you drag it in ___ your hole, drag it in your hole.

*Even traditional singers sometimes substitute "God bless" for dog-gone!

Old Ground Hog

Fast ♩ = 100

TENNESSEE

1. In, come Dad-dy from the plow In come Dad-dy
2. There's a piece of bread a- lay-ing on the shelf, There's a piece of bread a-
3. He picked up his gun and he whis-tled to his dog, He picked up his gun and he

from the plow: "I want some din-ner and I want it now"
lay-ing on the shelf, "If you get any more you'll get it your - self."
whis-tled to his dog — Off to the wild woods to ketch a ground hog.

Ground ____ hog.
Ground ____ hog.
Ground ____ hog.

4. Two in a rock and two in a log,
   Two in a rock and two in a log,
   Good lawdamercy, what a big ground hog.
       Ground hog.

5. Run here, Sal, with a ten-foot pole,
   Run here, Sal, with a ten-foot pole,
   Twist this ground hog out of this hole.
       Ground hog.

6. Daddy returned in a hour and a half, *(2 times)*
   He returned with a ground hog as big as a calf.
       Ground hog.

7. How them children whooped and cried, *(2 times)*
   I love that ground hog stewed and fried.
       Ground hog.

8. Took him home and tanned his hide, *(2 times)*
   Made the best shoe strings ever was tied.
       Ground hog.

9. Meat's in the cover and the hide's in the turn, *(2 times)*
   If that ain't ground hog, I'll be durn.
       Ground hog.

10. In come Sal with a snigger and a grin, *(2 times)*
    Ground hog gravy all over her chin.
        Ground hog.

11. Come here, Maw, and look at Sam, *(2 times)*
    He's et all the meat and sopping up the pan.
        Ground hog.

12. Old Aunt Sal was the mother of them all, *(2 times)*
    She fed them on ground hog before they could crawl.
        Ground hog.

Snake Baked a Hoecake

PENNSYLVANIA

Fast ♩ = 120

The snake baked a hoe-cake, and set the frog to watch it,

The frog fell a - doz-ing, and the liz-ard came and took it,

Bring back my hoe-cake, you long - tailed nan-ny - o.

Mole in the Ground

Fast ♩ = 132

NORTH CAROLINA

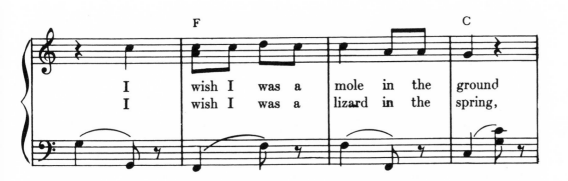

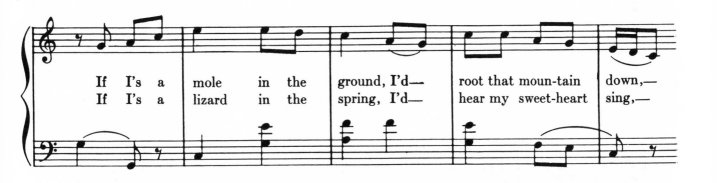

25

Little Dog Named Right

Moderately fast ♩ = 100

TENNESSEE

Verse

Had a lit - tle dog, his name was Right, Run the dev - il most ev - ery night,

Run him a - round the fod-der stack, My lit - tle dog he's nev-er got back.

REFRAIN

He's gone, he's gone, he's jes' keep a-get-tin' up gone,

He's gone, he's gone, he's jes' keep a-get-tin' up gone.

Little Lap-Dog Lullaby

COME UP, HORSEY

ALABAMA

Little Brown Dog

3. I buyed me a flock of sheep, I thought they were all wethers,
   Sometimes they yielded wool, sometimes they yielded feathers.
   I think mine are the best of sheep for yielding me increase,
   For every full and change of the moon they bring both lambs and geese.
       Sing taddle-o-day.

4. I buyed me a little box about four acres square,
   I fill-ed it with guinea and silver so fair.
   Oh, now I'm bound for Turkey, I'll travel like an ox,
   In my breeches pocket I'll carry my little box.
       Sing taddle-o-day.

Oh, Blue

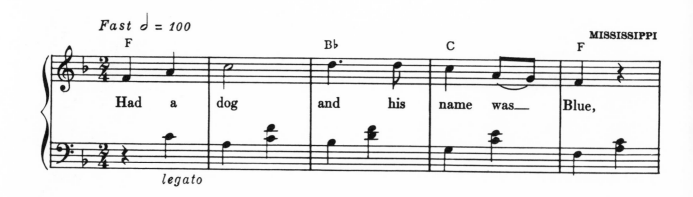

Fast ♩ = 100

MISSISSIPPI

Had a dog and his name was— Blue,

Bet your life he's a round-er, too,

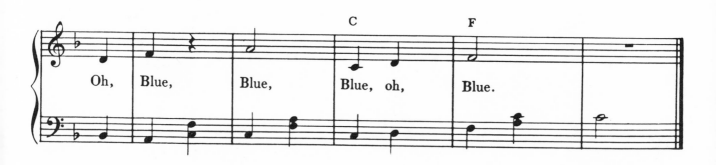

Oh, Blue, Blue, Blue, oh, Blue.

2. Every night just about good dark
   Blue goes out and begins to bark,
   Oh, Blue, Blue, Blue, oh, Blue.

3. Everything just in a rush,
   He treed a possum up a white-oak bush,
   Oh, Blue, Blue, Blue, oh, Blue.

4. Possum walked out on the end of a limb,
   Blue set down and talked to him,
   Oh, Blue, Blue, Blue, oh, Blue.

5. Blue got sick and very sick,
   Sent for the doctor to come quick,
     Oh, Blue, Blue, Blue, oh, Blue.

6. Doctor come and he come in a run,
   Says, "Old Blue, your hunting's done,"
     Oh, Blue, Blue, Blue, oh, Blue.

7. Blue died and he died so hard,
   Scratched little holes all around in the yard,
     Oh, Blue, Blue, Blue, oh, Blue.

8. Laid him out in a shady place,
   Covered him over with a possum's face,
     Oh, Blue, Blue, Blue, oh, Blue.

9. Dug his grave with a silver spade,
   Laid him down with a golden string,
     Oh, Blue, Blue, Blue, oh, Blue.

10. When I get to Heaven I think what I'll do,
    I'll take my horn and blow for Blue,
      Oh, Blue, Blue, Blue, oh, Blue.

Old Fox

Fast ♩ = 108

1. Old fox walked out one moon-shin-y night, On his two be-hind legs
2. He walked on down to the farm-er's gate And there he spied
3. Old drake set still and he cried out, "No! If you nev-er eat no meat

omit music under bracket in stanzas 3 and 5

and he took a might-y fight, Said, "I'll have some meat for my sup-per to-night,
an old black drake, Said, "Old black drake, come and go a-long with me,
till you eat me to-night, - - - - - - - - - - - - - - - - -

Be - fore I leave this old town-y-o.
I'm the hon - est old fel-low in this town-y-o.
You'll nev - er eat no meat in this town-y-o.

REFRAIN

This old town-y-o, this old town-y-o, Be - fore I leave this old town-y-o.
In this town-y-o, in this town-y-o, I'm the hon-est old fel-low in this town-y-o.
In this town-y-o, in this town-y-o, You'll nev-er eat no meat in this town-y-o.

4. He walked on down to the farmer's coop,
   And there he spied an old gray goose,
   Said, "Old gray goose, come and go along with me,
   I'm the honest old fellow in this towny-o,
      In this towny-o, in this towny-o,
      I'm the honest old fellow in this towny-o."

5. Old goose set still and she cried out, "No,
   If you never eat no meat till you eat me tonight,
   Omit music under bracket, proceeding from ★ to ★
   You'll never eat no meat in this towny-o.
      In this towny-o, in this towny-o,
      You'll never eat no meat in this towny-o."

6. Old fox stepped back and he gave a short stack,
   And he heaved the old gray goose by the neck,
   Her wings went flip-flop over his back,
   And her heels knocked ringle dingle darney-o,
      Dingle darney-o, dingle darney-o,
      And her heels knocked ringle dingle darney-o.

7. Old Mother Hippletoe a-lying in the bed
   Hoisted up the window and she popped out her head:
   "Old man, old man, the gray goose is gone,
   I think I heard her holler quing quarney-o,
      Quing quarney-o, quing quarney-o,
      I think I heard her holler quing quarney-o."

8. Old man jumped up by the light of the moon,
   With his pipe in his mouth and his britches in his hand,
   Said, "Old Father Fox, you'd better move away from here,
   You'll have some music behind you,
      Behind you, behind you,
      You'll have some music behind you."

9. He run the old fox into his den,
   Out come the young ones nine or ten,
   Said, "Old Father Fox, where have you been tonight,
   You're the heft'est old fellow in this towney-o,
      In this towney-o, in this towney-o,
      You're the heft'est old fellow in this towney-o."

10. Old fox run on into his den,
    There sat the young ones nine or ten,
    He carved the old goose without knife or fork,
    And the young ones sucked the bones-e-o,
       The bones-e-o, the bones-e-o,
       And the young ones sucked the bones-e-o.

33

The Deer Song

SALLY BUCK

NORTH CAROLINA

Fast ♩ = 120 F

1. On a bright and sum-mer's morn-ing, The ground all covered with snow,
2. I came a-cross a herd of deer, and I trailed them through the snow,

I put my shoul-der to my gun, And a-hunt-ing I did
I trailed them through the moun-tains Where straight up they did

And a-hunt-ing I did go.
Where straight up they did go.

Continue without pause

3. I went up yonder river
   That ran up yonder hill,
   And there I spied the herd of deer
   And in it they did . . .
   And in it they did dwell.

4. Soon as the buck they saw me,
   Like devils they did run
   To the bottom of the river
   And squat upon the . . .
   And squat upon the ground.

5. Then I went under water,
   Five hundred feet or more,
   I fired off my pistols,
   Like cannon they did . . .
   Like cannon they did roar.

6. I fired away among the buck,
   At length I kill-ed one,
   The rest stuck up their bristles,
   And at me they did . . .
   And at me they did come.

34

7. I fought them with my broadsword,
   Six hours I held them play,
   I killed three hundred and fifty,
   The rest they ran a- . . .
   The rest they ran away.

8. I gathered up my venison
   And out of waters went,
   To seek and kill all those that fled,
   It was my whole in- . . .
   It was my whole intent.

9. I bent my gun in a circle,
   And shot all round the hill,
   And out of five-and-twenty deer
   Ten thousand I did . . .
   Ten thousand I did kill.

10. I went up on the mountain,
    Beyond the peak so high,
    The moon come round with lightning speed,
    "I'll take a ride," says . . .
    "I'll take a ride," says I.

11. He carried me all round this world,
    All round the swelling tide,
    The stars they brought my venison,
    And so merrily I did . . .
    So merrily I did ride.

12. The moon came round the mountain,
    It took a sudden whirl,
    And my foot slipped and I fell out,
    And landed in this . . .
    And landed in this world.

13. The money that I got for
    The venison skin
    I hauled it to my daddy's barn,
    And it wouldn't half go . . .
    It wouldn't half go in.

And We Hunted and We Hunted

THREE JOLLY WELSHMEN

MISSOURI

Fast ♩ = 84

And we hunt-ed and we hunt-ed and we hunt-ed and we found

A pig in the lane and him we left be-hind — look-ee there!

Some said it was a pig, but oth-ers said nay,

Some said it was an el-e-phant with its snout shot a-way — look-ee there!

2. And we hunted and we hunted and we hunted and we found
   A frog in the well, and him we left behind—lookee there!
   Some said it was a frog, but others said nay,
   Some said it was a canary with his feathers washed away—lookee there!

3. And we hunted and we hunted and we hunted and we found
   A man in the road, and him we left behind—lookee there!
   Some said it was a man, but others said nay,
   Some said it was a monkey with his tail cut away—lookee there!

4. And we hunted and we hunted and we hunted and we found
   An owl in an ivy bush, and it we left behind—lookee there!
   Some said it was an owl, but others said nay,
   Some said it was the devil and we all ran away—lookee there!

One traditional singer said he knew upward of a hundred stanzas of this old nonsense song, made up around the lumber camp in which he learned the song. Favorite comparison among singers is that of the owl and the devil. Other comparisons heard in various parts of New England and the South, include:

A horse in the wood	— a deer, but its horns are shot away
A cat in the wood	— an owl, and its ears are shot away
The moon in the elements	— a cheese, but the half's cut away
A hedgehog	— a pincushion with the pins stuck in the wrong way
A girl in a cottage	— an angel with her wings blown away
A barn in the meadow	— a church with the steeple washed away
A ship in full sail	— a washtub with the clothes hung out to dry

Our own family adds new stanzas each evening:

A snake in the grass	— a branch with the twigs cut away
A ball in the road	— a turtle with its legs tucked away
A child in the bed	— a bear, and we all ran away
	or a pony gone to sleep on the hay
	or any number of other things

The Gray Goose

Fast ♩ = 132

E min   B min

1. It   was   last   Mon - day   morn - ing,   Lawd, lawd,   lawd,
2. Well, my   dad - dy went a - hunt - ing,   Lawd, lawd,   lawd,

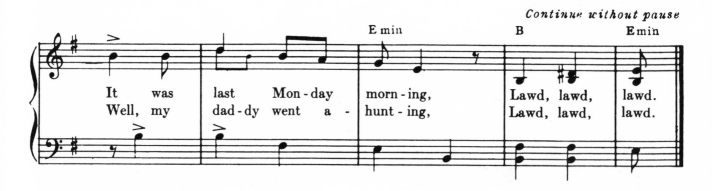

Continue without pause

E min   B   E min

It   was   last   Mon - day   morn - ing,   Lawd, lawd,   lawd.
Well, my   dad - dy went a - hunt - ing,   Lawd, lawd,   lawd.

ALTERNATE ACCOMPANIMENTS ad lib.

I

II

3. And he took along his shotgun,
   Lawd, Lawd, Lawd,
   And he took along his shotgun,
   Lawd, Lawd, Lawd.

4. Well, he spied a goose a-coming, *etc.*
5. Well, he threw his gun away up, *etc.*
6. And he rammed his hammer way back.
7. And the trigger went a-click-clack.
8. And the gun went a-boo-loo.
9. Well, he shot that old gray goose.
10. He was six months a-falling.
11. Well, they put him in the wagon.
12. Well, the wagon wouldn't hold him.
13. And they carried him to the white house.

14. Oh, it's your wife and my wife.
15. Well, they give a feather picking.
16. They were six months a-picking.
17. Well, they put him in the oven.
18. Well, the oven couldn't bake him.
19. And they put him on the table.
20. And the fork couldn't stick him.
21. Nobody couldn't eat him.

22. Well, they throwed him in the hog pen.
23. Well, the hogs couldn't eat him.
24. 'Cause he broke the sow's jawbone.
25. Well, they put him on a desert.
26. Well, the last time they seen him.
27. He was skipping 'cross the desert.
28. Crying a-quink quank, a-quink quank
29. Well, my father got angry.
30. Said the fire wouldn't cook him.
31. And my wife she couldn't cook him.
32. Oh, the mules couldn't pull him.
33. Been a old, old gray goose.
34. I'll a-never go to hunting.

Old Lady Goose

Moderate ♩ = 88

INTRODUCTORY REFRAIN *(may be repeated)*

Old la - dy goose, done turned her loose,
Old la - dy goose, old la - dy goose,

Where am that old la - dy goose, goose, goose, goose?

STANZAS

1. Looked down the pas - ture, looked down the lane,
2. I's just like that old la - dy goose,
3. Old la - dy goose just a - settin' in the pas - ture,

Can't find the old la - dy goose a - gain.
When - ev - er I is turned a - loose.
And I went down right there af - ter her.

REFRAIN

Old la - dy goose, goose, goose, goose, goose, Can

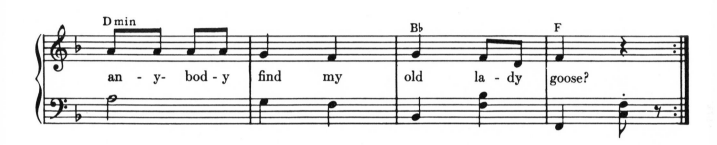

an - y- bod - y find my old la - dy goose?

The alto (down-stems) is also the tune of the third stanza. All stanzas can, however, be sung to the tune of the first stanza (up-stems).

The Old Hen Cackled and the Rooster Laid the Egg

Fast ♩ = 112

TEXAS

1. The old hen she cack-led, she cack-led in the loft,
2. The old hen she cack-led, she cack-led in the lot,

The next time she cack - led, she cack - led in the trough.
The next time she cack - led, she cack - led in the pot.

REFRAIN 1 (sung 3 times, or more)

D. C. for stanzas

The old hen she cack - led, she cack - led in the loft,
The old hen she cack - led, she cack - led in the trough,
The old hen she cack - led, she cack - led in the trough.

REFRAIN 2

The old hen she cack-led, she cack-led in the lot,

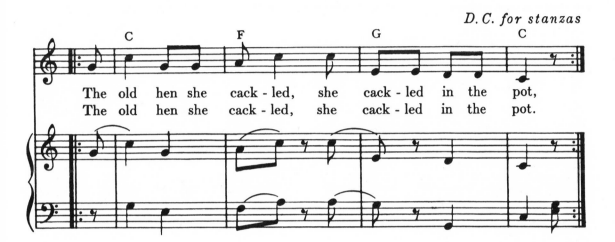

D.C. for stanzas

The old hen she cack-led, she cack-led in the pot,
The old hen she cack-led, she cack-led in the pot.

3. The old hen she cackled, she cackled in the stable,
The next time she cackled, she cackled on the table.

   REFRAIN:

   The old hen she cackled, she cackled in the stable,
   The old hen she cackled, she cackled on the table,
   The old hen she cackled, she cackled on the table.

4. The old hen she cackled and she cackled and she flew,
The old hen she cackled and the rooster cackled too.
Refrain:

5. The old hen she cackled, and the rooster laid the egg,
The old hen she cackled, and the rooster laid the egg.
Refrain:

Rhymes in the refrains do not follow a set pattern of repetition, and the music of the two refrains need not occur in any regular order in the singing of later stanzas.

43

My Old Hen's a Good Old Hen

CLUCK OLD HEN

My old hen's a good old hen, She lays eggs for the sec-tion men. (rail- road)

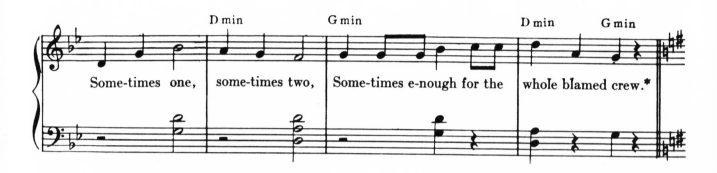

Some-times one, some-times two, Some-times e-nough for the whole blamed crew.*

REFRAIN

Cluck, old hen, cluck, I tell you, Cluck, old hen, or I'm a-going to sell you,

staccato

Cluck, old hen, cluck, I say, Cluck, old hen, or I'll give you a-way.

* To provide an indefinite number of stanzas, the old hen may lay "sometimes enough" for a variety of recipients, from "me and you" to "the baby (or the children or the circus or the president) too."

Turkey Song

WISCONSIN

The singer of this song just hummed the refrain, but she liked the nonsense syllables we were singing to it and asked us to publish them with her father's song. "My father had a habit of supplying any word or line when singing to us children. Mother has since told me some people sang the refrain

Godamighty bless the baby, Godamighty bless the baby-o,
Godamighty bless the baby, there ain't no use in talking.

but this version never reached the ears of us children."

Shake That Little Foot, Dinah-o

Fast ♩ = 100

Old Aunt Di - nah went to town Rid - ing a bil - ly goat, lead-ing a hound,

Shake that lit- tle foot, Di - nah - o, Shake that lit- tle foot, Di - nah - o.

TEXAS

2. Hound dog barked, billy goat jumped,
   Set Aunt Dinah straddle of a stump,
      Shake that little foot, Dinah-o,
      Shake that little foot, Dinah-o.

3. Sift the meal and save the bran.
   Give it to the old cow to make her stand,
      Shake that wooden leg, Dinah-o,
      Shake that wooden leg, Dinah-o.

4. Old Aunt Dinah sick in bed,
   Sent for the doctor, the doctor said
      Shake that little foot, Dinah-o,
      Shake that little foot, Dinah-o.

5. Get up, Dinah, you ain't sick,
   All you need is a hickory stick,
      Shake that little foot, Dinah-o,
      Shake that little foot, Dinah-o.

6. I like sugar in my coffee-o,
   The old folks they won't have it, no.
      Shake that wooden leg, Dinah-o,
      Shake that wooden leg, Dinah-o.

There Was an Old Frog

Fast ♩ = 112

ARKANSAS

There was an old frog and he lived in the spring, Ching-a chang-a pol-ly mitch-a cow-me-o,

He was so hoarse he could-n't sing, Ching-a chang-a pol-ly mitch-a cow-me-o.

REFRAIN

Kee-mo ky-mo do-ro war, May-hi, may-lo, my rump-side, pull ma-dell,

Pen-ny-win-kle, soap butt, link-horn, nip-cat, Ching-a chang-a pol-ly mitch-a cow-me-o.

2. I grabbed him by the leg and pulled him out,
   Ching-a chang-a polly mitch-a cow-me-o,
   He hopped and he skipped and he bounced all about,
   Ching-a chang-a polly mitch-a cow-me-o.

   REFRAIN:
   Kee-mo ky-mo do-ro war,
   May-hi, may-lo, my rump side, pull-ma-dell,
   Penny-winkle, soap butt, link horn, nip cat,
   Ching-a chang-a polly mitch-a cow-me-o.

3. Cheese in the spring house nine days old,
   Ching-a chang-a polly mitch-a cow-me-o,
   Rats and skippers is a-getting mighty bold,
   Ching-a chang-a polly mitch-a cow-me-o.
   Refrain:

4. Big fat rat and a bucket of souse,
   Ching-a chang-a polly mitch-a cow-me-o,
   Take it back to the big white house,
   Ching-a chang-a polly mitch-a cow-me-o.
   Refrain:

Little Pig

Fast ♩ = 112

Man and a wo-man bought a lit-tle pig,— M, m, m,

Man and a wo-man bought a lit-tle pig,

Did-n't cost much, for it was-n't ver-y big,— M, m, m.

50

2. Little piggy did a lot of harm, M, m, m,
   Little piggy did a lot of harm,
   Rooting all about the farm, M, m, m.

3. Little piggy died for the want of breath, M, m, m,
   Little piggy died for the want of breath,
   Wasn't that an awful death, M, m, m.

4. Man and a woman weeps and cried, M, m, m,
   Man and a woman weeps and cried,
   Then they both lay down and died, M, m, m.

5. Here they lay one-two-three, M, m, m,
   Here they lay one-two-three,
   Man and a woman and little pig-gee, M, m, m.

6. Here they lay all on the shelf, M, m, m,
   Here they lay all on the shelf,
   If you want any more you can sing it yourself, M, m, m.

51

The Old Sow

THE MEASLES IN THE SPRING

What will we do with the old sow's hide?

Make as good cush-ion as ev - er did ride.

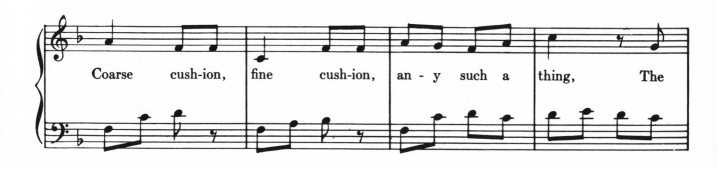

Coarse cush-ion, fine cush-ion, an - y such a thing, The

old sow died with the meas-les in the spring.

ARKANSAS

2. What will we do with the old sow's tail?
   Make as good whip as ever did sail.
   Coarse whip, fine whip, any such a thing,
   The old sow died with the measles in the spring.

   3. What will we do with the old sow's meat?
      Make as good bacon as ever was eat.
      Coarse bacon, fine bacon, any such a thing,
      The old sow died with the measles in the spring.

      4. What will we do with the old sow's feet?
         Make as good pickles as ever was eat.
         Coarse pickles, fine pickles, any such a thing,
         The old sow died with the measles in the spring.

5. What will we do with the old sow's head?
   Make as good oven as ever baked bread.
   Coarse oven, fine oven, any such a thing,
   The old sow died with the measles in the spring.

Disposing of other parts of the sow can make this a long song — her bones, marrow, knuckles, snout ("as fine a shaker as shakes salt out," says an 8-year-old), her knees, legs, ears, hair, side ("best old bacon that ever was fried") — even her squeal.

The Little Black Bull

HOOSEN JOHNNY

ILLINOIS

Moderately fast ♩ = 104

The lit-tle black bull came down the mea-dow, Hoo-sen John-ny, Hoo-sen John-ny,

The lit-tle black bull came down the mea-dow, Long time a - go.

REFRAIN

Long time a - go, Long time a - go,

The lit-tle black bull came down the mea-dow, Long time a - go.

54

2. First he paw and then he bellow,
   Hoosen Johnny, Hoosen Johnny,
   First he paw and then he bellow,
   Long time ago.

   REFRAIN:
   Long time ago,
   Long time ago,
   First he paw and then he bellow,
   Long time ago.

3. He whet his horn on a white-oak sapling,
   Hoosen Johnny, Hoosen Johnny,
   He whet his horn on a white-oak sapling,
   Long time ago.

   REFRAIN:
   Long time ago,
   Long time ago,
   He whet his horn on a white-oak sapling,
   Long time ago.

4. He shake his tail, he jar the meadow, *etc.*

5. He paw the dirt in the heifers' faces, *etc.*

The Old Cow Died

SAIL AROUND

The old cow ___ died, Sail - a -round, The old cow ___ died, Sail a -round.

1. Did you give her hot wa-ter? Yes, ma'am. Did you give her an-y so-da? Yes, ma'am.
2. Did you send for the doc-tor? Yes, ma'am. Did the doc - tor come? Yes, ma'am.

REFRAIN:
The old cow died, Sail around,
The old cow died, Sail around.

3. What 'n the world's ailed her? Yes, ma'am.
Did she die of the cholera? Yes, ma'am.
Refrain:

4. Did the buzzards come? Yes, ma'am.
Did the buzzards eat her? Yes, ma'am.
Refrain:

5. Did they sail high? Yes, ma'am.
Did they sail low? Yes, ma'am.

REFRAIN:
The old cow died, Sail around,
The old cow died, Sail around.

A group of children dance or skip around the "old cow," wings flop-ping—sometimes acting out such stanzas as 4 or 5, sometimes inventing new ones.

Black Sheep, Black Sheep

SOUTH CAROLINA

Moderately fast ♩ = 144

Black sheep, black sheep, where's your lamb? Way down in the val - ley,

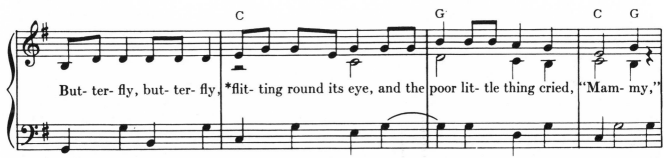

But - ter - fly, but - ter - fly, *flit - ting round its eye, and the poor lit - tle thing cried, "Mam - my,"

Mam - my said when she went a - way, to take good care of the ba - by, When

she come back she'd bring a piece of cake, and give a lit - tle bit to the ba - by.

* Traditional singers often sing buzzards and the butterflies "pecking at" or "picking out."

The Big Sheep

THE RAM OF DARBY

TENNESSEE

Moderately fast ♩ = 100

1. As I went to mar-ket, On one mar-ket day
2. Oh, he was so big, sir, He could nei-ther walk nor stand,
3. Oh, the first tooth he had, sir, Was big as a sad-dle horn,

I saw as big a sheep, sir, as ev - er fed on hay.
And ev - ery foot he had, sir, It cov-ered an acre of land.
The next one — to it, Held for - ty barrels of corn.

REFRAIN

Oh, fare - a - rad - dy dad-dy, Oh, fare - a - rad - dy day,

Oh, fare - a - rad - dy dad-dy, Oh, fare - a - rad - dy day.

REFRAIN:
Oh, fare-a-raddy daddy, oh, fare-a-raddy day,
Oh, fare-a-raddy daddy, oh, fare-a-raddy day.

4. Oh, the wool on his belly, it dragged to the ground,
   The devil cut a piece out to make his wife a gown.
   Refrain:

5. And the wool on his back, sir, it reached to the sky,
   The eagles built their nest there, I heard the young ones cry.
   Refrain:

6. Oh, this sheep he had two horns, sir, they reached up to the moon,
   A man went up in January and never got down till June.
   Refrain:

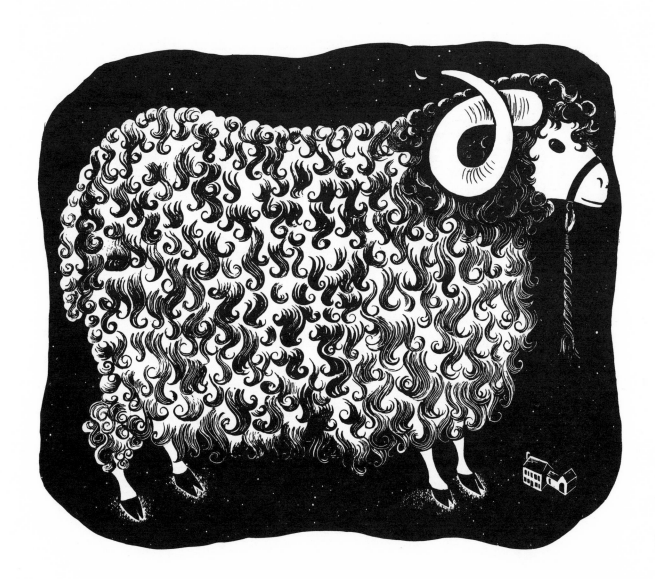

Old Bell'd Yoe

INTERLUDE 1 (fiddle)

Fast ♩ = 108

KENTUCKY
D min
F

STANZA

F

Oh, the old bell'd yoe 'n' the lit - tle speck-led weth-er,

Run-ning down the hill with their tails tied to-geth-er.

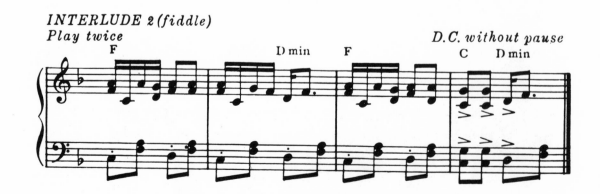

INTERLUDE 2 (fiddle)
Play twice

D.C. without pause

F   D min   F   C   D min

2. Oh, the old bell'd yoe and the little speckled wether—
The fence fell down and the sheep's gone together.

3. Oh, the old bell'd yoe and the bell without a clapper—
I'd give five dollars to see Fannie Napper.

* *"Yoe" is this singer's pronunciation for "ewe." A wether is a ram.
"Napper" is a favorite name for dogs: Fannie Napper is undoubtedly
the sheep dog.*

The Kicking Mule

Refrains need not be sung after each stanza.

3. This mule he am a kicker,
   He's got a iron back,
   He headed off a Texas railroad train
   And kicked it clear of the track.

4. You see that mule a-coming,
   He's got about a half a load,
   When you see a roomy mule,
   Better give him all the road.

   ALTERNATE REFRAIN:
   Whoa there, mule, I tell you,
   Well, whoa there, mule, I say,
   Just keep your seat, Miss Liza Jane,
   And hold on to that sleigh.

5. Went to see Miss Dinah one morning,
   She was bent all over her tub,
   And the more I'd ask her to marry me,
   Well, the harder she would rub.
   Refrain:

6. Well, I went down to the huckleberry picnic,
   Dinner all over the ground,
   Skippers in the meat was nine foot deep,
   And the green flies walking all around.

7. The biscuit in the oven was a-baking,
   Was a beefsteak frying in the pan,
   Pretty gal sitting in the parlor,
   Good Lawdamighty, what a hand I stand.
   Refrain:

Whoa, Mule! Can't Get the Saddle On

Moderately fast ♩ = 96

A min

ALABAMA

1. Whoa, mule! Can't get the sad-dle on, Whoa, mule! Can't get the sad-dle on.
2. Catch that mule! Can't get the sad-dle on, Catch that mule! Can't get the sad-dle on.
3. Ride that mule! Can't keep the sad-dle on, Ride that mule! Can't keep the sad-dle on.

4. Run, mule! Can't keep the sad-dle on, Run, mule! Can't keep the sad-dle on.
5. Run, mule! Can't keep the sad-dle on, Run, mule! Can't keep the sad-dle on.

legato

Go to Sleep

BUY A PRETTY PONY

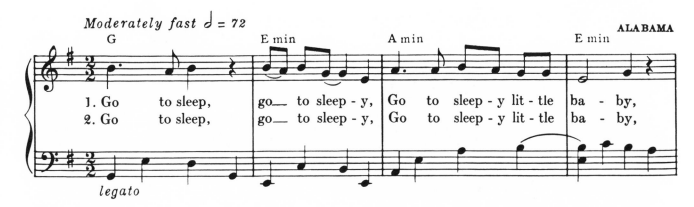

3. Go to sleep, go to sleepy,
   Go to sleepy, little baby,
   Catch a pony and saddle him up,
   Ride all over this pasture.

The singer of this song, Florida Hampton, actually ends stanza 1:
   Hush, li'l baby, and don't you cry,
   Do, the bugger-bear catch you.

and another stanza:
   Mammy run away, Daddy wouldn't stay,
   Left nobody but the baby.

Harriet McClintock, also of Alabama, sings:
   Mama gone away, and daddy too,
   For to get the baby little rabbit.

and Frank Galloway of Texas:
   When you wake, give you pattercake
   And roast you sweet potato.

But usual promises are of cake, and of ponies, horses, or mulies:
   When you wake you'll have some cake
   And all the mulies in the stable.

65

Hop Up, My Ladies

VIRGINIA

Fast ♩ = 112

1. Did you ev- er go to meet-in', Un- cle Joe, Un-cle Joe?
2. Will your horse carry doub - le, Un- cle Joe, Un-cle Joe?

ramp ad lib.
staccato
staccato

Did you ev - er go to meet- in', Un-cle Joe? Did you ev - er go to meet-in', Un-cle
Will your horse car-ry dou - ble, Un-cle Joe? Will your horse car-ry dou - ble, Un-cle

Joe, Un - cle Joe? Don't mind the wea - ther, so the wind don't blow.
Joe, Un - cle Joe? Don't mind the wea - ther, so the wind don't blow.

REFRAIN

Hop up, my la-dies, three in a row, Hop up, my la - dies, three in a row,

Continue without pause

Hop up, my la-dies, three in a row, Don't mind the wea-ther, so the wind don't blow.

REFRAIN:
Hop up, my ladies, three in a row,
Hop up, my ladies, three in a row,
Hop up, my ladies, three in a row,
Don't mind the weather, so the wind don't blow.

3. Is your horse a single-footer, Uncle Joe, Uncle Joe?
   Is your horse a single-footer, Uncle Joe?
   Is your horse a single-footer, Uncle Joe, Uncle Joe?
   Don't mind the weather, so the wind don't blow.
   Refrain:

4. Would you rather own a pacer, *etc.*

5. Say, you don't want to gallop, *etc.*

6. Say, you might take a tumble, *etc.*

7. Well, we'll get there soon as the others, *etc.*

Stewball

MISSISSIPPI

When Stewball *is sung as a work song the stanzas are usually sung by a leading singer, the group joining in with him on "uh huh" or on echoes of final portions of lines. These group comments have been indicated here by italics.*

3. There's a big bell, *uh huh*, for to tamp on, *uh huh*,
   For them horses, *uh huh*, to run, *to run*,
   Young ladies, *uh huh*, young gentlemen, *uh huh*,
   From Balti-, *uh huh*, -more come, *-more come*,
       -More come, man, *uh huh*, -more come, *-more come*.

4. 'Way out in, *uh huh*, Kentucky, *uh huh*,
   Where old Stewball, *uh huh*, come from, *come from*,
   It got stamped in, *uh huh*, put in the paper, *uh huh*,
   That he blowed down, *uh huh*, in a storm, *in a storm*,
       In a storm, man, *uh huh*, in a storm, *in a storm*.

5. Well his bridle, *uh huh*, was silver, *uh huh*,
   And his saddle, *uh huh*, was gold, *was gold*,
   And the price on, *uh huh*, his blanket, *uh huh*,
   Hasn't never, *uh huh*, been told, *been told*,
       Been told, man, *uh huh*, been told, *been told*.

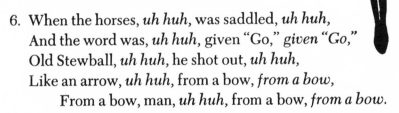

  6. When the horses, *uh huh*, was saddled, *uh huh*,
      And the word was, *uh huh*, given "Go," *given "Go,"*
      Old Stewball, *uh huh*, he shot out, *uh huh*,
      Like an arrow, *uh huh*, from a bow, *from a bow*,
         From a bow, man, *uh huh*, from a bow, *from a bow*.

    7. Well the old folks, *uh huh*, they hollered, *uh huh*,
        And the young folks, *uh huh*, they bawl, *they bawl*,
        But the li'l children, *uh huh*, just look-a-look, *uh huh*,
        At the noble, *uh huh*, Stewball, *Stewball*,
           Stewball, man, *uh huh*, Stewball, *Stewball*.

8. Well old Stewball, *uh huh*, were a-scrambling, *uh huh*,
   Up that nine-mile, *uh huh*, high hill, *high hill*,
   Well that jockey, *uh huh*, looked behind him, *uh huh*,
   And he spied old, *uh huh*, Wild Bill, *Wild Bill*,
       Wild Bill, man, *uh huh*, Wild Bill, *Wild Bill*.

  9. Old Molly, *uh huh*, was a-climbin', *uh huh*,
      That great big, *uh huh*, long lane, *long lane*,
      And she said to, *uh huh*, her rider, *uh huh*,
      Can't you slack that, *uh huh*, left rein, *left rein*,
         Left rein, man, *uh huh*, left rein, *left rein*.

    10. The races, *uh huh*, they ended, *uh huh*,
         And the judges, *uh huh*, played the band, *played the band*,
         And old Stewball, *uh huh*, beat Molly, *uh huh*,
         Back to the, *uh huh*, grand-stand, *grand-stand*,
           Grand-stand, man, *uh huh*, grand-stand, *grand-stand*.

Riding Round the Cattle

WHOOP-TI-YIDDLE-UM-YEA

Fast ♩ = 96
INTRODUCTION (first time only)

TEXAS

Whoop-ing up cat-tle, I'm set-ting up strad-dle, I'm rid-ing round the cat-tle,

REFRAIN

Fine

And a whoop-ti- yid-dle-um yea, yum-a yea, And a whoop-ti- yid-dle-um day.

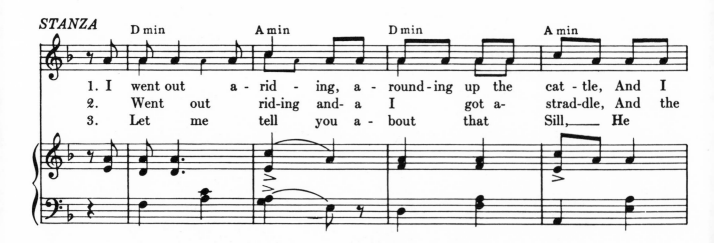

STANZA

1. I went out a- rid - ing, a - round-ing up the cat - tle, And I
2. Went out rid-ing and- a I got a- strad-dle, And the
3. Let me tell you a - bout that Sill,___ He

70

thought I would be a - rid - ing up strad-dle,
mule throwed me right back off of the sad - dle,
throwed me right at the foot of the hill,___

REFRAIN:
And a whoop-ti-yiddle-um-yea yum-a-yea,
And a whoop-ti-yiddle-um-day

Since this song is closely related to the Old Chisholm Trail, *any of several hundred stanzas may be sung to it.*

My foot in the stirrup, my seat in the saddle,
I'm the best little cowboy that ever rode a-straddle.

I'm on my best horse and I'm going at a run,
I'm the quickest-shooting cowboy that ever pulled a gun.

Oh, my foot's in the stirrup and my hand's on the horn,
I'm the best durn cowboy that ever was born.

With my blankets and my slicker and my rawhide rope,
I'm a-sliding down the trail in a long keen lope.

Oh, a ten-dollar horse and a forty-dollar saddle,
And I'm going to punching Texas cattle.

It's cloudy in the west and looking like rain,
And my darned old slicker's in the wagon again.

I woke up one morning on the old Chisholm Trail
With a rope in my hand and a cow by the tail.

My seat in the saddle, and I gave a little shout,
The lead cattle broke and the herd ran about.

I'm up every morning before daylight,
And before I sleep the moon shines bright.

Crocodile Song

Fast ♩. = 132

NOVA SCOTIA

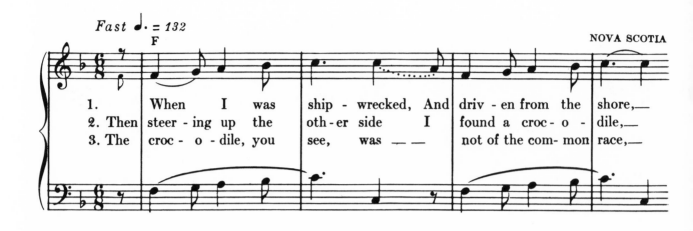

1.
When I was ship - wrecked, And driv - en from the shore, ___

2. Then steer - ing up the oth - er side I found a croc - o - dile, ___

3. The croc - o - dile, you see, was ___ not of the com - mon race, ___

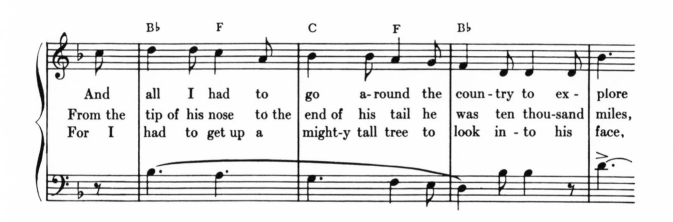

And all I had to go a - round the coun - try to ex - plore

From the tip of his nose to the end of his tail he was ten thou - sand miles,

For I had to get up a might-y tall tree to look in - to his face,

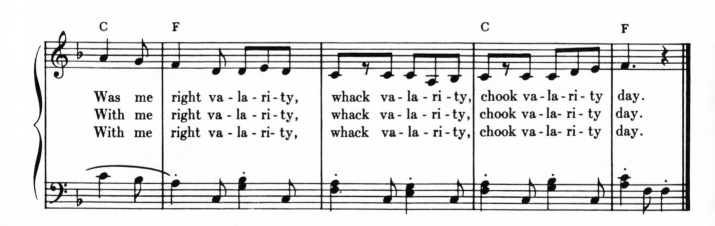

Was me right va - la - ri - ty, whack va - la - ri - ty, chook va - la - ri - ty day.

With me right va - la - ri - ty, whack va - la - ri - ty, chook va - la - ri - ty day.

With me right va - la - ri - ty, whack va - la - ri - ty, chook va - la - ri - ty day.

4. I bore away from his head one day
   With every stitch of sail,
   And going nine knots by the log
   In ten months reached his tail.
       With a right valarity, whack valarity,
       Chook valarity day.

5. The wind was blowing hard
   And blowing from the south,
   The tree it broke and down I fell
   Into the crocodile's mouth,
       With me right valarity, whack valarity,
       Chook valarity day.

6. The crocodile he set his mouth,
   And he thought he had his victim,
   But I went down his throat, you see,
   And that is how I tricked him
       With a right valarity, whack valarity,
       Chook valarity day.

7. I roamed about his throat
   Until I found his maw,
   And there was bullocks' heads and hearts
   Laid up there by the store,
       With a right valarity, whack valarity,
       Chook valarity day.

8. The crocodile was getting old
   And shortly after died,
   It took me six months and forty-two days
   To work a hole up through his side
       With me right valarity, whack valarity,
       Chook valarity day.

9. Come all you fellows, come listen to me,
   If ever you travel the Nile,
   'Tis where I fell you will see the shell
   Of the wonderful crocodile,
       With me right valarity, whack valarity,
       Chook valarity day.

Go On, Old 'Gator

The sign × indicates hammer beats heard on the recording of this work song.

Of All the Beast-es

I'D RATHER BE A PANTHER

Of all the beast-es in the world, I'd ra-ther be a pan-ther

I'd crawl up-on some lone-some hill, __ And cry __ for Su-si-an-na

The following stanza comes from Alabama. In both stanzas, "panther" is pronounced "panner."

2. Of all the beast-es in the world
   I'd rather be a panther,
   Eat all the chickens down the line
   And turkeys in Atlanta.

Jack, Can I Ride?

SEE THE ELEPHANT JUMP THE FENCE

REFRAIN:
Jack, can I ride? Ho, ho,
Jack, can I ride? Ho, ho,
Jack, can I ride? Ho, ho,
Jack, can I ride? Ho, ho.

3. Jaybird sitting on a swinging limb,
   Winked at me and I winked at him,
   Picked up a stick and I hit him on the shin,
   "Good Lawdamighty, don't do that again.'
   Refrain:

   REFRAIN:
   Jack, can I ride? Ho, ho,
   Jack, can I ride? Ho, ho,
   Jack, can I ride? Ho, ho,
   Jack, can I ride? Ho, ho.

The Alabama singer calls this a clapping song. Another singer ends stanza 3:
   Says he, "You better not do that again."

Daddy Shot a Bear

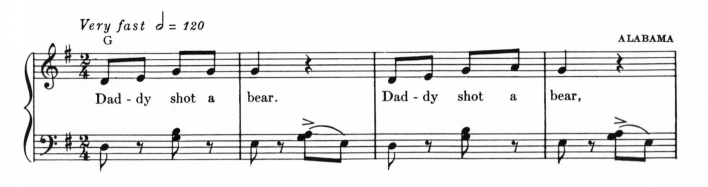

Very fast ♩ = 120

ALABAMA

Dad - dy shot a bear. Dad - dy shot a bear,

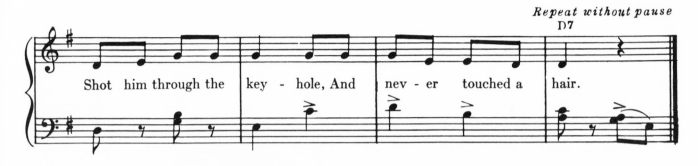

Repeat without pause
D7

Shot him through the key - hole, And nev - er touched a hair.

Wolves A-Howling

MISSISSIPPI

Fast ♩ = 116

REFRAIN

Oh, wolves are howl-ing, howl-ing, howl-ing, Oh, them wolves are howl-ing,

Fine

howl-ing, howl-ing.

STANZA

Wolves is a-howl-ing, holl'-ring a-round my poor lit-tle dar-ling,

D.C. without pause

See them blue clouds a-fly-ing, my poor lit-tle dar-ling's at home and a-cry-ing.

In the refrain the left hand plays the fiddle tune which accompanies the song on the record.

Animal Song

MICHIGAN

Al-li-ga-tor, hedge-hog, ant-eat-er, bear, Rat-tle-snake, buf-fa-lo, an-a-con-da, hare.

2. Bullfrog, woodchuck, wolverine, goose,
   Whippoorwill, chipmunk, jackal, moose.

3. Mud turtle, whale, glow-worm, bat,
   Salamander, snail, and Maltese cat.

4. Black squirrel, coon, opossum, wren,
   Red squirrel, loon, South Guinea hen.

5. Polecat, dog, wild otter, rat,
   Pelican, hog, dodo, and bat.

6. Eagle, kingeron, sheep, duck, and widgeon,
   Conger, armadillo, beaver, seal, pigeon.

7. Reindeer, blacksnake, ibex, nightingale,
   Martin, wild drake, crocodile, and quail.

8. House rat, toe rat, white bear, doe,
   Chickadee, peacock, bobolink, and crow.

80